Disney's TARZAN®

Terk's Tale

Adapted by Eric Suben

Illustrated by Kim Raymond, painted by Philippe Harchy
Cover illustration by Judith Clarke, Denise Shimabukuro, painted by Andrea & John Alvin

A GOLDEN BOOK • NEW YORK

Golden Books Publishing Company, Inc., New York, New York 10106

Hey! I'm Terk. (My real name's Terkina, but I only let my mom call me that.) One of my best buddies is a hairless wonder named Tarzan. Okay, I'll admit it. Sometimes he can be a pest and he's always gettin' into trouble.

One time he ran smack into our leader, Kerchak! Kerchak wasn't happy.

Seeing as how the kid needed help, I ran right up and
acted like I was looking for Tarzan.
"Oh, thank you, thank you so much for finding him,
Kerchak," I said, layin' it on real thick.
"You are such a wise and caring leader."

We got out of there pretty quick.

"How many times do I have to tell ya?" I asked Tarzan.

"Stay away from Kerchak!"

Just then my pals Flynt and Mungo raced by.

"Hey, come on, Terk!" shouted Flynt.
"Last one there's a dung beetle," cried Mungo.
I wanted to go hang out with them. But I didn't
need Tarzan taggin' along. The other guys
thought he was weird.

"Terk, can I come?" Tarzan asked.

"Well, yeah, you could, if you could keep up," I told him.

"But ya know, ya can't really keep up." And I took off so fast that I left him far behind.

"The fun has arrived!" I announced as I caught up with Flynt and Mungo. "I had a little pest-control problem, but it's all taken care of."

At least that's what I thought . . .

SLAM! Tarzan landed right on my back. "Terk said I could come along if I could keep up," he said.

"Oh, no!" groaned the others. "Terk, come on!"

"I'll handle this, guys, okay?" I told them.

"Personally, I'd love to hang out with you," I said, takin' Tarzan aside. "But the guys, they need a little convincing, ya know?"

"Okay. What do I gotta do?" Tarzan asked.

"Uh . . . you gotta get a hair," I told him. "An elephant hair."

I thought Tarzan would go straight home. Wouldn't you? I mean, those elephants are huge! But he was determined and zipped right past me.

"Tarzan! Nooooo!" I cried. But he jumped right off the cliff, yellin' his head off.

For the longest time, Tarzan was under the water. Then I spotted him.
"Hey, guys!" he shouted as he popped up to the surface.

"Oh, no, no, no, no, no! Come back! Come back!" I yelled when I saw
him swimming toward the elephants. I was afraid that Tarzan was
gonna get hurt—and I was gonna get in big trouble.

As we watched, Tarzan came up right near an elephant. The idiot was tryin' to pluck a hair from the elephant's tail!

I guess those elephants never saw an animal like Tarzan. "Piranha!" screamed a little elephant. Then they all started freakin' out and shoutin', "Piranha!"

And that's when it happened—the elephant stampede! CRASH! The elephants thundered into the jungle, smashin' the trees and headin' right for my family, who were enjoyin' a termite picnic. It was pretty scary, but I had scarier things to worry about. Most of all, I was worried about Tarzan.

When the dust cleared, I ran down to the lagoon and dragged Tarzan out of the water. "Tarzan, buddy," I said. "Don't die on me! I didn't really think you'd do it."

"Get away from there!" someone cried from behind me. "Don't you know that a piranha can strip your flesh in seconds?" It was Tantor, the nutty little elephant who had started the stampede.

Suddenly, Tarzan sat up! Man, was I glad he was alive. But was I
ever mad at him! "You nearly gave me a heart attack!" I told him.
"Hey, Terk," he said, "I got the hair!"

The stampede was over, and our whole family rushed over to see if everyone was okay. Kerchak came, too. And was he furious!

"What happened?" Kerchak demanded.

"Um . . . well . . ." I started to explain, "it's sort of a long—"

Suddenly Tarzan stepped forward. "It was my fault, Kerchak," he said. "We were playing. I'm sorry. It was an accident."

That's when I knew that the hairless kid was all right. Maybe Tarzan was little and weird. But he was pretty brave, too.

From that day on we were best friends. Together we would
always have great times in the jungle—Tarzan, me, and our
new pal, Tantor!